BENEFITS FORGOT

LECTOR HOUSE PUBLIC DOMAIN WORKS

This book is a result of an effort made by Lector House towards making a contribution to the preservation and repair of original classic literature. The original text is in the public domain in the United States of America, and possibly other countries depending upon their specific copyright laws.

In an attempt to preserve, improve and recreate the original content, certain conventional norms with regard to typographical mistakes, hyphenations, punctuations and/or other related subject matters, have been corrected upon our consideration. However, few such imperfections might not have been rectified as they were inherited and preserved from the original content to maintain the authenticity and construct, relevant to the work. The work might contain a few prior copyright references as well as page references which have been retained, wherever considered relevant to the part of the construct. We believe that this work holds historical, cultural and/or intellectual importance in the literary works community, therefore despite the oddities, we accounted the work for print as a part of our continuing effort towards preservation of literary work and our contribution towards the development of the society as a whole, driven by our beliefs.

We are grateful to our readers for putting their faith in us and accepting our imperfections with regard to preservation of the historical content. We shall strive hard to meet up to the expectations to improve further to provide an enriching reading experience.

Though, we conduct extensive research in ascertaining the status of copyright before redeveloping a version of the content, in rare cases, a classic work might be incorrectly marked as not-in-copyright. In such cases, if you are the copyright holder, then kindly contact us or write to us, and we shall get back to you with an immediate course of action.

HAPPY READING!

BENEFITS FORGOT

HONORÉ WILLSIE (HONORÉ MORROW)

ISBN: 978-93-5420-775-4

Published: -

© 2021
LECTOR HOUSE LLP

LECTOR HOUSE LLP
E-MAIL: lectorpublishing@gmail.com

**"COME HERE AND SIT DOWN AND WRITE A LETTER
TO YOUR MOTHER!"**

—*Page 74.*

BENEFITS FORGOT

A STORY OF LINCOLN AND MOTHER LOVE

BY

HONORÉ WILLSIE

AUTHOR OF "STILL JIM," "LYDIA OF THE PINES," ETC.

**WITH ILLUSTRATIONS BY
CHARLES E. CARTWRIGHT**

CONTENTS

I

THE DONATION PARTY

Brother Meaker rose from his pew and looked at Jason appraisingly.

"I don't know, brethren," he said. "Of course, he's a growing boy. Just turned twelve, didn't you say, ma'am?" Jason's mother nodded faintly without looking up, and Brother Meaker went on. "As I said, he's a growing boy, but he's dark and wiry. And I've always noted, the dark wiry kind eat smaller than any other kind. I should take at least twelve pounds of sugar off the allowance for the year and four gallon less of molasses than you was calculatin' on."

He sat down and Sister Cantwell rose. She was a fat woman, famous in the southern Ohio country for the lavish table she set.

"Short sweetening," she said in a thin high voice, "is dreadful high. I said to Hiram yesterday that the last sugar loaf I bought was worth its weight in silver. I should say, cut down on short sweetening. Long sweetening is all right except for holidays."

Jason whispered to his mother, "What's long sweetening, mother?"

"They must mean molasses," she whispered in return, with a glance at Jason's father, who sat at the far end of the pew reading his Bible as he always did at this annual ordeal.

Jason looked from his mother's quiet, sensitive face, like yet so unlike his own, to the bare pulpit of the little country church, then back at Brother Ames, who was conducting the meeting. This annual conference and the annual donation party were the black spots in Jason's year. His mother, he suspected, suffered as he did: her face told him that. Her tender lips, usually so wistful and eager, were at these times thin and compressed. Her brown eyes, that except at times of death or illness always held a remote twinkle, were inscrutable.

Jason's face was so like, yet already so unlike his mother's! The same brown eyes, with the same twinkle, but tonight instead of being inscrutable, boyishly hard. The same tender mouth, with tonight an unboyish sardonic twist. What Jason's father's face might have said one could not know, for it was hidden under a close-cropped brown beard. He turned the leaves of his Bible composedly, looking up only as the meeting reached a final triumphant conclusion with Brother Ames' announcement:

"So, Brother Wilkins, there you are, a liberal allowance if I must say it. Two hundred and fifty dollars for the year, with the usual donation party to take place in the fall of the year."

Brother Wilkins, who was Jason's father, rose, bowed and said: "I thank you, brethren. Let us pray!"

The fifty or sixty souls in the church knelt, and Jason's father, his eyes closed, lifted his great bass voice in prayer:

"O God, You have led our feeble and trusting steps to this town of High Hill, Ohio. You have put into the hearts and minds of these people, O God, the purpose of feeding and clothing us. Whether they do it well or ill, concerns them and You, O God, and not us. We are but Your humble servants, doing Your divine bidding. Yet this is perhaps the proper occasion, Our Heavenly Father, to thank You that You have sent us but one child and that unlike Solomon, Your servant has but one wife. And now, O God, bless these people in their giving. And make me, in my solitary circuit riding in the hills and valleys a proper mouthpiece of Your will. For Lord Jesus' sake, Amen."

There was a short pause after the rich voice stopped, then a few weak "Amens" came from different corners of the church and Brother Ames, jumping to his feet, exclaimed:

"Let us close the meeting by singing

'How tedious and tasteless the hours
When Jesus no longer I see—'"

This ended Jason's first day at High Hill. The salary was small, even for a Methodist circuit rider, in the decade before the Civil War. It was smaller by fifty dollars than what they had been allowed the year before. Yet, High Hill, as Mrs. Wilkins pointed out to Jason the next day, was much more attractive than any town they had been in for years. There was a good school, and the Ohio river-packet stopped twice a week, and a Mr. Inchpin in the town was reported to be the owner of a number of books. Jason's mother was an Eastern woman and sometimes the loneliness and hardship of her life made her find solace in what seemed to Jason inconsequential things. Still, he was glad of the school, for he was a first-class student and already had decided to take his father's and mother's advice that he study medicine. And the packet, warping in twice a week, was, after all, something to which one might look forward and Mr. Inchpin's books would be wonderful.

Jason was sure that the Ohio valley in which he had spent the whole of his short life was the most beautiful spot in the world. The lovely green heights rolling back into the Kentucky sky line, were, he thought, great enough for David, whose cattle fed upon a thousand hills. The fine headlands on the Ohio side, wooded, mysterious, were, he was sure, clad in verdure like the utmost bound of the everlasting hills of Jacob. And High Hill with its fifteen hundred souls was "a city, builded on a hill that could not be laid."

For Jason was brought up on the Bible. His father believed that it ought to be, outside of his school text books, his only literature. His mother, with her Eastern traditions, thought otherwise. A Methodist circuit rider before the Civil War moved every year, and every year Mrs. Wilkins combed each new community for books. It was wonderful how she and Jason scented them out.

They had been in High Hill about a week when Jason came panting into the house late one afternoon. His father was writing a sermon in the sitting room. Jason tip-toed into the kitchen, where his mother was preparing supper.

"The packet's in, mother, and I carried a man's carpet bag up to the hotel and look—what he gave me!"

His slender boyish brown hands fairly trembled as he held a torn and soiled magazine toward his mother. She dropped the biscuit she was molding and seized it.

"*Harper's Monthly!* O Jason dear, how wonderful! You shall read it aloud to me after supper."

"It's prayer meeting night," said Jason in a sick voice.

His mother flushed a little. "So it is! My goodness, Jason! Print makes a heathen of me and you're most as bad. You haven't fed the horse or milked."

"So I won't get a look at it till tomorrow," cried Jason, bitterly.

Mrs. Wilkins glanced toward the closed door that led into the sitting room. Then she looked at Jason's wide brown eyes, at the round-about she had cut over from his father's old sermon coat, at the darned stockings and the trousers that had belonged to the rich boy of the town they had lived in the year before.

"Jason," she said, "you ought to get plenty of sleep because you're a growing boy. But a thing like this won't happen for years again—and—well, I've saved up several candle ends, hoping to get some sewing done nights when your father was using the lamp. When you go up to bed tonight, take those and read your magazine."

"But you ought to keep them," protested Jason.

"Not at all," exclaimed his mother, vigorously, "it's all for your education. Run along now and milk."

So Jason reveled in his *Harper's Monthly*, and the next day as he wiped the dishes for his mother, he produced his great idea.

"If I can earn the money, this summer, mother, can I subscribe to *Harper's Monthly* for a year?"

"My goodness, Jason, it's five dollars and this is the first of August! School begins in a month."

"I know all that," replied Jason impatiently, "but if I earn the money can I have it for *Harpers Monthly*?"

"Of course you can. It's all for your education, my dear. I never forget that."

A money paying job for a boy of twelve was a hard thing to find in High Hill and Jason was late for supper that night. But his brown eyes were shining with triumph when he slid into his seat and held out his bowl for his evening meal of mush and milk.

"I've got a job," he said.

"A job?" queried his father. He smiled a little at Jason's mother.

"Yes, sir. Mr. Inchpin is having a new barn built on the hill back of his house. The brook runs at the foot of it and I'm going to haul gravel and sand and water up to the building site. It'll take about a month. He provides the horse and wagon."

"And how much will he pay you?" asked Mrs. Wilkins.

"He says he can't tell till he's through. But I'm going to ask him for five dollars."

Jason's father looked amused and a little troubled. "Jason, I hope you're not too interested in Mammon. But I must say I'm glad to see you have your mother's energy."

"Or your father's," said Mrs. Wilkins, smiling into the blue eyes opposite hers. "Nobody can say that a circuit rider lacks energy."

And so during the hot August days, Jason toiled on Mr. Inchpin's new barn, never once visiting the swimming hole in the brook, never once heeding the long-drawn invitation of the cicada to loll under the trees with one of Mr. Inchpin's books, never once breaking away when the toot of the packet reverberated among the hills.

"He's a fine lad," Mr. Inchpin told Jason's father. "I never have seen such determination in a little fellow."

Brother Wilkins looked gratified, but when he repeated the little compliment to Jason's mother he added, "I don't believe I understand Jason altogether."

"I do," said Mrs. Wilkins, stoutly.

August came to an end with cool nights and shorter days and Mr. Inchpin's barn was finished of a Saturday evening. He called Jason into the house, into the library where there were bound volumes of *Godey's Lady's Book* and Blackwood, and handed him three paper dollars.

"There you are, my man. I'd intended to give you only two. But you've done well, by ginger, so here's three dollars."

Jason looked up at him dumbly, mumbled something, stuffed the bills into his trousers pocket and bolted for home. He burst in on his mother in the kitchen, buried his face against her bosom and sobbed.

"I can't have it after all! He only gave me three dollars! I can't have it! And now I'll never know how that story 'Bleak House' ended."

Jason's father came into the kitchen, hastily: "What in the world —"

"Jason! Jason! don't sob so!" cried Mrs. Wilkins. "We'll raise the rest of the money some way. I'll find it. Hush, dear, hush! Mercy, the mush is burning!"

Jason's father took the boy's grimy blistered hand, such a strong slender hand and so like his mother's, and sitting down in the kitchen chair, he pulled Jason to him.

"Tell me, Jason," he urged gently, "what money?"

Jason still torn with occasional sobs, managed to tell the story.

"*Harper's Monthly*," exclaimed Brother Wilkins. "Dear! Dear! I had hoped you'd give the money to a foreign mission, Jason."

"Foreign mission!" cried Jason's mother. "Well, I guess not! Jason's education is going to be taken care of before the heathen."

"But how'll we get the extra dollars?" asked Brother Wilkins, helplessly.

"I'll manage," replied Jason's mother, her gentle voice a little louder than usual.

"Then let us eat supper," said Jason's father, clearing his throat for grace.

Jason's mother sold a girlhood treasure, a little silver-tipped hair-pin, to the storekeeper's wife, the following Monday, for two dollars, and the jubilant Jason exchanged the single bills for a single note. The note was cut in two and sent in separate letters to New York, this being the before the war method of safeguarding loss of money in the mail. There was a period of several weeks of waiting during which Jason met every mail. Then a third letter was sent by Jason's mother, asking why the delay, and telling Jason's little story.

Jason met the return packet, his heart now high, now low. He had met so many futile packets since the first of September. But this time there was a letter explaining that but one-half of the note had arrived in New York, but that on faith, the editors were sending the back numbers of the magazine requested and that the rest of the year's subscription would follow. And Jason never did know whether or not the second half of the note arrived.

And there they were, a fat pile of magazines! Jason clasped them in his arms and rushed home with them. A tag tail of boys followed him and by nightfall most of the town knew that Jason Wilkins had four numbers of *Harper's Monthly* on hand.

Jason was out milking the cow when Mr. Inchpin arrived.

"Heard Jason had some new magazines in hand. Don't s'pose you could lend me a few, over night?"

Jason's mother was in the kitchen. It was donation party night and she had been cooking all day in preparation.

"Surely, surely," said Jason's father, picking up the pile of magazines. "Jason can't get at them before the end of the week. Take them and welcome."

Mr. Inchpin rode away. Jason came in with the milk pail and the family sat down to a hasty supper.

"Won't I have a minute of time to look at my magazines, mother?" asked Jason. "O, I hate donation parties!"

"Jason!" thundered his father. "Would you show ingratitude to God? And the books are not here anyway. I loaned them to Mr. Inchpin."

"Father!"

"O Ethan!"

Brother Wilkins' eyes were steel gray, instead of blue. "Jason can read his Bible until the end of the week. His ingratitude deserves punishment."

Jason rushed from the table and flung himself sobbing into the hay loft. His mother found him there a few moments later.

"I know, dear! I know! It's hard. But father doesn't love books as you and I do, so he doesn't understand. And you must hurry and get ready for the party."

"I don't want the donation party, I want my magazines," sobbed Jason.

"I know. But life seldom, so very seldom, gives us what we want, dear heart. Just be thankful that you will be happy at the end of the week and come and help mother with the party."

As donation parties go, this one was a huge success. Fully a hundred people attended it. They played games, they sang hymns, they ate a month's provisions and Mrs. Wilkins' chance of a new dress in the cake and coffee she provided. They left behind them a pile of potatoes and apples that filled two barrels and a heap of old clothing that Jason, candle in hand, turned over with his foot.

"There's Billy Ames' striped pants," he grumbled. "Every time his mother licked him into wearing 'em, I know he prayed I'd get 'em, the ugly beasts, and I have. And there's seven old patched shirts. I suppose I'll get the tails sewed together into school shirts for me and there's Old Mrs. Arley's plush dress—I suppose poor mother'll have to fix that up and wear it to church. Why don't they give stuff father'll have to wear, too? I wonder why a minister's supposed to be so much better than his wife or son."

"What's that you're saying, Jason?" asked his father sharply as he brought the little oil lamp from the sitting room into the kitchen. Mrs. Wilkins followed. This was a detestable job, the sorting of the donation debris, and was best gotten through with, at once. Jason, shading the candle light from his eyes, with one slender hand, looked at his father belligerently.

"I was saying," he said, "that it was too bad you don't have to wear some of the old rags sometimes, then you'd know how mother and I feel about donation parties."

There was absolute silence for a moment in the little kitchen. A late October cricket chirped somewhere.

Then, "O Jason!" gasped his mother.

The boy was only twelve, but he had been bred in a difficult school and was old for his years. He looked again at the heaps of cast-off clothing on the floor and his gorge rose within him.

"I tell you," he cried, before his father could speak, "that I'll never wear another donation party pair of pants. No, nor a shirt-tail shirt, either. I'm through with having the boys make fun of me. I'll earn my own clothes every summer and I'll earn mother's too."

"You'll do nothing of the sort, sir," thundered Jason's father, his great bass voice rising as it did in revival meetings. "You'll do nothing but wear donation clothes as long as you're under my roof. I've long noted your tendency to vanity and mammon. To my prayers, I shall begin to add stout measures."

Jason threw back his head, a finely shaped head it was with good breadth between the eyes.

"I tell you, sir, I'm through with donation pants. If folks don't think enough of the religion you preach to pay you for it I'd—I'd advise you to get another religion."

Under his beard, Ethan Wilkins went white, but not so white as Jason's mother. But she spoke quietly.

"Jason, apologize to your father at once."

"I couldn't accept an apology now," said the minister. "I shall have to pray to get my mind into shape. In the meantime Jason shall be punished for this. Not until everyone in the town who desires to read his *Harper's Monthlies* has done so, can Jason touch them."

"O father, not that," cried Jason. "I'll apologize! I'll wear the pants! Why, it would be Christmas before I'd see them again!"

"I can't accept your apology now. Neither your spirit nor mine is right. And I cannot retract. Your punishment must stand."

Jason was all child now. "Mother," he cried, "don't let him! Don't let him!"

Mrs. Wilkins' lips quivered. For a moment she could not speak. Then with an inscrutable look into her husband's eyes she said:

"You must obey your father, Jason. You have been very wicked."

Jason put down his candle and sobbed. "I know it. But I'll be good. Let me have my magazines. They're mine. I paid for them."

"No!" roared the minister. "Go to bed, sir, and see to it that you pray for a better heart."

Jason's sobs sounded through the little house long after his father and mother had gone to bed. The minister sighed and turned restlessly.

"Why was I given such a rebellious son, do you suppose?" he asked finally.

"Perhaps God hopes it'll make you have a better understanding of children," replied Mrs. Wilkins. "Christ said that unless you became like one of them you could not enter the kingdom."

There was another silence with Jason's sobs growing fainter, then, "But he was wicked, Mary, and he deserved punishment."

"But not such a punishment. Of course, I had to support you, no matter what I thought. But O Ethan, Ethan, it's so easy to kill the fineness in a proud and sensitive heart like Jason's."

"Nevertheless," returned the minister, "when he spurns the giving hand of God, forgiveness is God's, not mine. We'll discuss it no more."

Nor was the matter discussed again. Jason appeared at breakfast, with dark rings about his eyes, after having done his chores, as usual. Once, it seemed to his mother that he looked at her with a gaze half wondering, half hurt, as if she had failed him when his trust and need had been greatest. But he said nothing and she hoped that her mind had suggested what was in her aching heart and that Jason's was only a child's hurt that would soon heal.

He never again asked for the magazines. On Christmas morning his father placed them, tattered and marred, from their many lendings, beside his plate. Jason did not take them when he left the table and later on his mother carried them up to his room. Whether he read them or not, she did not know. But she was glad to see him begin again to watch for the packet and read the current numbers as they arrived.

She dyed Billy Ames' striped pants in walnut juice and they really looked very well. Jason wore them without comment as he did the shirts she fashioned for him from many shirt tails.

And in the spring they left High Hill for a valley town.

II

THE CIRCUIT RIDER

The years sped on with unbelievable swiftness as they are very prone to do after the corner into the teens is turned.

Jason worked every summer, but he did not offer to buy his mother a dress nor did he buy himself either clothing or books. He put all he earned by toward his course in medicine. When he was a little fellow, his mother had given him a lacquered sewing box that had belonged to her French mother. It had proved an admirable treasure box for childish hoardings. Jason, the summer he was thirteen, cleared it out and put into it his summer earnings, ten dollars.

With his newly acquired reticence, he did not speak of the box, nor did he mention the extra bills, quarters and dollars that appeared there from time to time. The little hoard grew slowly, very slowly, in spite of these anonymous additions — it grew as slowly as the years sped rapidly, it seemed to Jason's mother.

Jason must have been sixteen, the summer he went with his father on one of the Sunday circuit trips. He never had been on one before. But it had been decided that he was to begin his medical studies in the fall. He was to be apprenticed to a doctor in Baltimore and his mother was anxious for father and son to draw together if possible before the son went into the world. Not that Jason and the minister quarreled. But there never had been the understanding between the two that except for the unfortunate magazine episode, always had existed between Jason and his mother.

The trip lay in the hills of West Virginia. Brother Wilkins rode his old horse, Charley, a handsome gray. Jason rode an old brown mare, borrowed from a parishioner for the trip.

Mrs. Wilkins, standing in the door, watched the two ride off together with a thrill of pride. Jason was almost as tall in the saddle as his father. He had shot up amazingly of late. The minister was getting very gray. He had been late in his thirties when he married. But he sat a horse as though bred to the saddle and Old Charley was a beauty. Brother Wilkins was very fond of horses and was a good judge of horse flesh. Sometimes Mrs. Wilkins had thought, that if Ethan had not chosen to be a Methodist minister he would have made a first-class country squire.

She watched the two out of sight down the valley road, then with a little sigh turned back to the empty home.

Jason, though always a little self-conscious when alone with his father, was delighted with the idea of the trip. They crossed the Ohio on the ferry and rode rapidly into the West Virginia hills. The minister made a great effort to be entertaining and Jason was astonished at his father's intimate knowledge of the countryside.

"I don't see how you remember all the places, father," he said at noon, when the minister had turned to a side road to find a farmer whom he wished to greet.

"I had this circuit years ago before you were born, my boy. I know the people intimately."

"Don't you get tired of it?" asked Jason, suddenly.

"Tired of saving souls?" returned his father. "Do you think you'll ever get tired of saving bodies?"

"O that's different," answered the boy. "You've got something to take hold of, with a body."

"And the body ceases to exist when the soul departs. Never forget that, my boy."

"But you work so hard," insisted Jason, "and you get so little for it. I don't mean money alone," flushing as if at some memory, "but it doesn't seem as if the people care. They'll take all they can get out of each minister as he comes along, and then forget him."

Brother Wilkins looked at Jason, thoughtfully. "Sixteen is very young, Jason. I'm afraid you were born carnal minded. I pray every night of my life that as you grow older, you'll grow toward Christ and not away from Him."

Again Jason flushed uncomfortably and a silence fell that lasted until they reached the remote hill settlement where service was to be held that night. The settlement consisted of a log church, surrounded by a scattered handful of log houses, each already with its tiny glow of light, for night comes early in the hills. The two had eaten a cold lunch in the saddles, for church service would begin as soon as they arrived.

There were twenty-five or thirty people in the rough little church. They crowded round Brother Wilkins enthusiastically when he entered and he called them all by name as he shook hands with them. Jason slid into a back seat. His father mounted to the pulpit.

"Let us open by singing

'How tedious and tasteless the hours
When Jesus no longer I see—'"

The old familiar tune! Jason wondered how many meetings his father had opened with it. The audience sang it with a will. In fact with too much will. A group of young men on the rear seat opposite Jason sang with unnecessary fervor, quite drowning out the female voices in the congregation. Jason saw his father, his face heavily shadowed in the candle-light, glance askance at the rear seat.

"Let us pray," said Brother Wilkins. There was a rustle as the congregation knelt. "O God, I have come to You again in this mountain place after many years and many wanderings. I thank You for giving me this privilege. I have greeted old friends who have not forgotten me and who all these years have remembered You and Christ, Your only begotten Son. Tonight, O Heavenly Father, I have brought with me to this sacred fold my own one lamb that he might see how sacred and how great is Your power. Look on him tonight, O Supreme Master, and mark him for Your own. And remember, that if the young men in the rear seat plan any disturbance tonight, O Heavenly Father, that the arm of Thy priest is strong and the soul of Thy servant is resolute. For Jesus Christ's sake, Amen."

The boom of "Amens" from the back seat was tremendous. Brother Wilkins, rising after his prayer, looked at the four young men for a long moment, over his glasses. Then he said:

"Let us sing

'From Greenland's icy mountains
To India's coral strands.'"

This was sung with tremendous vim, and the minister began his sermon. Jason's father was a good preacher. His vocabulary was rich and his ideas those of a thinking man whose religion was a passion. But the young men on the rear seat were unimpressed. One of them snored. Brother Wilkins stopped his sermon.

"Be silent, ye sons of Satan," he thundered. There was silence and he took up the thread of his talk. A low cat call interrupted him. The minister stopped and slipped off his coat, folding it carefully as he laid it on his desk. It was old and the seams would not stand strain. He rolled up his cuffs as he descended from the pulpit, the congregation watching him spell-bound. Jason had seen his father in action before and was deeply embarrassed but not surprised.

Brother Wilkins strode up to the pew where the offenders sat and seized by the ear the largest of the group, a hulk of twenty-one or so, larger than the minister. He led the young man into the aisle and reached up and boxed his ears, with the sound of impact of a club on an empty barrel.

"Now leave this house of God," roared the minister. The young fellow sneaked out the door. Brother Wilkins turned back to the pew.

"Don't you tech me or I'll brain ye," cried the youth who was about Brother Wilkins' own size.

"Hah!" snorted the minister. There was the sound of blows, a quick scuffling of feet and the second offender was booted out of the door. The remaining two made a quick and unassisted exit. Breathing a little heavily, Brother Wilkins returned to his sermon; and to his hypnotized and immensely regaled congregation it seemed that the rest of his preaching was as from one inspired by God.

Jason sat brooding deeply. Something within him revolted at the spectacle of his father descending from the pulpit to beat recalcitrant members of his congregation. An old and familiar sense of shame enveloped him, and he was thankful when once again darkness had enveloped them and they were traveling rapidly along the mountain road. They were to have a late supper and spend the night at a cabin well along the road they must travel on the morrow.

Brother Wilkins was in the abstracted state that always followed his preaching and Jason was glad to respect his silence, until it had lasted so long that he became uneasy.

"Father, didn't you say that Herd's was five miles beyond the church?"

The minister pulled up his horse. In the darkness Jason could barely see the outlines of his body.

"Heavens, Jason! Why didn't you rouse me sooner? This isn't the main traveled road. When did we leave it?"

"I don't know, sir. I thought you knew this part of the country so well—"

"So I do, ordinarily. But I can't recognize by-paths on a night like this. Wait, isn't that a light up the mountainside yonder? Come along, my boy, we'll find out where we are."

The light glowed only faintly from the open door of a cabin. An old woman, with a pipe in her mouth, sat crooning over a little fire in the crude fireplace. She looked up in astonishment when the two appeared in the doorway.

"Why, it's Brother Wilkins!" she cackled. "Lord's sake, what you doin' clar up hyar!"

"Why, Sister Clark! I am glad to see you," exclaimed Jason's father, shaking one of the old woman's hands, and shouting into her other, which she cupped round her ear. "My son and I must have got off the main road five miles back. We're on our way to Milton."

Sister Clark was visibly excited. "Ye ain't going on a step tonight. I can fix a shake-down for ye. Thing like this don't happen to a lone old woman twice in a lifetime. Bring in your saddle-bags—but Lord!" she stopped aghast. "I ain't got a bit of pork in the house, nor there ain't a chicken on the place. All I got is corn-meal and molasses."

"Plenty, Sister Clark! Plenty! Get the saddle-bags, Jason, and tie the horses to graze."

They ate their supper by candle-light after their hostess had cooked the mush in a kettle hanging from the crane. Brother Wilkins had a violent choking fit during the meal and Sister Clark pounded him on the back, apologizing as she did so for her familiarity with the minister.

Jason slept profoundly on his share of the shake-down that night, and at dawn, after more mush, they were up and away.

Twice on this day, Sunday, Brother Wilkins held service in the mountains and it was nine o'clock at night when they started toward the Ohio again. It was not until they had reached the river at dawn and had roused the ferryman that the minister recovered from his Sunday abstraction.

"Did you have a pleasant trip, Jason?" he asked as they led the horses into the boat.

"Yes, father," answered Jason dutifully.

Brother Wilkins looked at the boy, as if he were beholding him from a new angle.

"You don't look as much like your dear mother as you did in your childhood, my boy. Sometimes—I wonder—Jason, do you think this life has been too hard on your mother?"

"Yes, sir, I do. It's hard on a boy, why shouldn't it be doubly hard on a woman?"

The minister sighed. "Your reply is hardly polite, Jason, though I suppose my question merited it." Then with sudden heat: "Never mistake this cold frankness of yours for courage, my son. It takes more courage usually to be courteous than to be impolite. Did you notice that I coughed violently yesterday evening at Sister Clark's?"

"Yes, sir."

"Well, the cause of it was this. She went down to the spring and fetched a pail of water for the mush. When I was eating my helping, I felt a lump in my mouth. But the old lady had her eye on me every minute for fear I wouldn't enjoy the frugal meal, so I could only investigate with my tongue. I found that she had cooked a little bit of a frog in the mush. Now, Jason, if she had discovered that she never would have recovered from the mortification. The only time in her life the minister stopped with her. So, though it made me choke, I swallowed it. That, sir, is my idea of courtesy. I wish you not to forget it."

Jason's cool, speculative young gaze was on his father's face as he answered:

"I understand, father."

The minister turned away. "No, you don't. I doubt if you ever do." And he did not speak again until they reached home.

III

WAR

And so Jason went away to study medicine. He worked very hard and progressed very rapidly. By the time he was twenty he was no longer "the doctor's boy." He was a real assistant in all but fees. He had no share in the doctor's income and always was desperately hard up.

At first, he did not ask his father and mother for help. He did all sorts of odd chores to pay his way. But as he progressed in his profession, he had less and less time for earning his up-keep and had finally to write home for money. His mother always answered his letters and she never failed to send him money when he asked for it. How she managed it, Jason never asked. Perhaps he was ashamed to know.

In all these four years he did not come home. He would have liked to but the trip was prohibitively expensive.

Late in the fall of 1861, he received a letter from his mother containing a ten-dollar bill. It was a short letter. "Your father can't live more than a week. Come at once."

Jason put his head down on that letter and sobbed, then dried his eyes and sought the doctor, who loaned him the rest of the money needed for the trip.

The minister's circuit had swung him round again to High Hill. Jason disembarked from the packet late one November afternoon, carrying his carpet bag. Even in November, High Hill was beautiful. Through his sadness, Jason again felt the thrill of the giant headlands, the thousand hills of his boyish imaginings.

There was the same little cottage, more weather-beaten than he had remembered it. His mother was waiting for him at the door. The four years had changed her, yet she seemed to Jason more beautiful than his mental picture of her had been.

She kissed him with trembling lips. "He's still with us," she whispered. "I'm sure he waited for you."

"What is the matter with him?" asked Jason, huskily, as he deposited his carpet bag on the sitting-room table.

"Lung fever. He took a bad cold a month ago coming home from West Virginia in the rain. He was absent-minded, you know. If it hadn't been for Pilgrim, I don't think he'd ever got here."

"Pilgrim?" asked Jason, warming his hands at the fire.

"Surely I've written you about Pilgrim. Father bought him soon after you left. He's the wisest horse that ever lived. If you're warm, now, Jason, come to your father."

He followed her into the bedroom which opened off the kitchen. His father lay on the feather bed, his eyes closed. O how worn—O how changed! Young Jason was hardened to suffering and death. He had not realized that to the sickness and death of one's own, nothing can harden us. He stood breathing hard while his mother stooped over the bed.

"Ethan," she said softly, "our boy is here."

Brother Wilkins opened his eyes and smiled faintly. He tried to say something and Jason sprang to take his hand.

"Oh, he wants to speak to you and can't. O my poor dear! O Ethan, my dearest."

Jason's mother broke down. Jason put his finger on his father's wrist.

After a long moment, "Mother, he's gone," he whispered.

After the funeral, Jason wandered about the village for a day or so, trying to plan for his mother's future and his own. All the townspeople were kind to him.

"Haven't forgot how you loaned me those *Harper's Monthlies* before you read 'em yourself," said Mr. Inchpin. "Anything I can do for you or your mother, let me know."

The two had met in Hardwich's store, which was also the post office and the evening club for the males of High Hill. Jason had dropped in to post a letter.

A tall scraggly man joined in. "Your father was the best preacher in Ohio. We was all glad when he got back here."

"He had the gift of prayer," said an old man, in the back of the store.

There was a silence which Jason struggled in vain to break.

Then a young fellow who carried a buggy whip and smoked a cigar said, "How does the doctoring go, Jason?"

"Well, thanks," returned Jason, looking at the young fellow, intently. It was Billy Ames, he of the striped pants.

Back through Jason's heart, until now strangely softened by the happenings of the past few days, surged the accumulated bitterness of his poverty-stricken youth. He turned abruptly and left the store.

His mother was watching for him, anxiously. "Jason, Pilgrim had an accident. He's got a frightful cut on his right fore shoulder. He must have got caught on a nail somehow."

"Let's have a look at him," said Jason.

The big gray was standing stolidly in his stall. Mrs. Wilkins held the candle while Jason examined him. On the right fore shoulder was a great three-cornered tear from which the skin hung in a bloody fold.

"I'll have to sew it up." Jason was all surgeon now. "Do you think he'll stand still for us?"

"Stand still," replied Jason's mother, indignantly. "Why, he'll know exactly what you are doing, and why."

"All right then. You get me some clean rags and a darning-needle and I'll get the rest of the things I'll need."

In a few moments the operation was well in hand.

Pilgrim kept his ears back and his eyes on his mistress. He breathed heavily, but otherwise he did not stir. He was a large horse, with a small, intelligent head and a mighty chest. Jason's mother held the candle with one hand while she stroked the big gray's nose with the other.

"Be careful, Jason, do!" she said softly.

Jason grunted. "You keep him from biting or kicking and I'll do my share," he said.

"Pilgrim bite!" cried Jason's mother indignantly.

Again Jason grunted, working swiftly, with the skill of trained and accustomed fingers. The candle flickered on his cool young face, on his black hair and on his long, strong, surgeon's fingers. It flickered too on his mother's sweet lips, on her tired brown eyes and iron-gray hair. It put high-lights on the cameo at her throat and made a grotesque shadow of her hoop-skirts on the stable wall.

Finally Jason straightened himself with a sigh and wiped his hands on a towel.

"That's a good job," he said. "Must be some bad spikes here or in the pasture fence to have given him that rip. I'll hunt them up tomorrow.—Get over there!"

This last to Pilgrim, who suddenly had put his head on Jason's shoulder with a soft nuzzling of his nose against the young doctor's cheek and a little whinny that was almost human.

"Why, Jason, he's thanking you!" cried his mother. "He'll never forget what you've done for him tonight."

Jason gave the horse a careless slap and started out the stable door.

"You'll be having it that he speaks Greek next," he said.

"You don't know him," replied Jason's mother. "This is the first time you ever saw him, remember. These last three years of your father's life he's been like one of the family." She followed Jason into the cottage. "Often and often before your poor father died he said he'd never have been able to keep on with the circuit-riding and the preaching if he'd had to depend on any other horse than Pilgrim. That horse just knew father was forgetful. He wouldn't budge if father forgot the saddle-bags. When Pilgrim balked, father always knew he'd forgotten something and he'd go back for it. I'll have supper on by the time you've washed up, Jason."

The little stove that was set in the fireplace roared lustily. The kettle was singing. The old yellow cat slept cozily in the wooden rocker on the patch-work cushion. All the furniture, so simple and worn, was as familiar to Jason as the back of his hand.

Jason washed at the bench in the corner, then sat down while his mother put the supper before him—fried mush, fried salt pork, tea and apple sauce.

"Well," said Jason soberly, "what are we going to do now, mother? Father's gone and—"

His mother's trembling lips warned him to stop.

"It doesn't seem possible," she said, "that it's only a week since we laid him away."

Jason interrupted gently. "I know, mother; but you and I have got to go on living!"

"It's you I'm worrying about," said his mother.

"I've been wondering if you hadn't better come back to Baltimore with me," mused Jason. "I can eke out a living somehow for the two of us."

"No," said Mrs. Wilkins decidedly. "You've got burden enough to take care of yourself. I can get along till you're doctoring for yourself. Mr. Inchpin will let me have the cottage near the wharf if I'll go up to his house and cook his dinner for him. Then with a little sewing and a little nursing here in the village, the cow, the chickens and Pilgrim, I can get along. But I don't see how I can send you anything, Jason."

Jason had brightened perceptibly. "If I can just get through this year, mother, I'll be on my feet. But I've got to pay Dr. Edwards back. He's a hard driver. If we can get together enough for that, I'll manage, somehow."

Jason's mother sighed. "It does seem as if, all through the years, I ought to have saved something, but I haven't, not a cent, except what I raked and scraped together for your doctoring. Two hundred and fifty dollars a year beside donation parties is quite a sum, Jason, and I feel guilty that I haven't saved anything for you. But it all went, especially after father got sickly. I've sold a lot of things, Jason, so as to send you the money. I'm most at my wit's end now. Grandma's silver teapot, that kept you three months, and your father's watch, nearly six. That's the way the things have gone. My, how thankful I was we had 'em."

Jason was still so very like his mother, so very unlike. Where her face was sweet and tremulous, his was cool and still. His brown eyes were careless and yet eager. Hers were not inscrutable now. The light had gone out of them from weeping. Jason's long, strong hands were smooth and quiet. Hers were knotted and work calloused and a little uncertain.

As if something in her words irritated him, Jason said quickly, "Well, what did you and father start me on this doctor idea for, if you thought it was going to cost too much?"

"O, Jason, you know that thought never occurred to either of us! There are still some things to go that I've sort of hung on to. Take the St. Bartholomew candlestick to Mr. Inchpin. That will give you the money you need right now."

Jason looked up at the queerly wrought silver candlestick that was more like an old oil lamp than a candlestick. His mother's people had brought it from France with them. The family legend was that some Huguenot ancestor had come through the massacre of St. Bartholomew with this only relic of his home wrapped in his bosom.

"Good!" said Jason eagerly. "The old thing is neither fish nor flesh, anyhow. Too big mouthed for a candle and folks are going to use coal oil more and more, anyhow. I can be off tomorrow."

"Tomorrow's Thanksgiving, Jason."

"I'll be glad to forget it," grumbled Jason. "What have we to be thankful for?"

His mother looked at him a little curiously, but she said nothing. Jason caught the expression in her eyes.

"Don't look at me that way, mother," he burst forth angrily, "I can't forgive father, with his big brain and body for doing so little for you and me. I can't forgive him for what he dragged us through—those donation parties! He had no right to put me through what he did that year at High Hill. And what did he get out of his life? They lay him away with the remark that he had a gift of prayer! And his widow may starve, for all of them."

"Jason, be silent," cried his mother. She had risen and stood facing him, her face deathly white. "Not one word against your father. Because you never could appreciate him, you needn't belittle him now. Not one word," as Jason would have spoken. "He was my husband and I loved him, God knows. O Ethan, Ethan, how shall I finish my span of years alone!" she broke down utterly.

Jason put his arms about her. "Mother, I didn't mean to hurt you. Truly I didn't. It's only that—" he stopped and set his lips tightly while he petted her in silence.

"I pray, Jason," said his mother, finally, "that you will never have a grief or a punishment great enough to soften your heart."

Jason did not answer. He went up to see Mr. Inchpin that night, and the following day started back East again.

IV

MR. LINCOLN

Three times a week during the year that followed, Jason's mother saddled Pilgrim and rode him to the post office after the shrieks of the whistle had warned her that the tri-weekly packet had come and gone. Four times during the year she heard from Jason.

"April 3, 1862.

"Dear Mother:

"I am very well indeed, and hope that you are not overworking. Things are not going very well here. Everybody is hard pressed because of the war and Dr. Edwards simply can't make any collections. We get a good many soldiers who are sent home half cured and, of course, we get nothing at all from them—don't want to, in fact. Is there any way we could raise just a little money? Not a cent that you've earned, understand, but perhaps you could sell your old mahogany hat-box. Mrs. Chadwick always wanted it. I never did care for those old things and I don't think you do. After I get started in practice, I'll buy you a dozen hat-boxes. Won't it be great when you can come down here and live with me?

"Your loving son,
"JASON."

"June 7, 1862.

"DEAR MOTHER:

"I have been quite sick with a sore hand—almost got gangrene from a soldier. That's why you haven't been hearing from me. I received the ten dollars. Thank you very much. I didn't think the old trap would bring that much. Dr. Edwards said yesterday that I had a genius for surgery. The ten dollars paid my board for six weeks, giving me a chance to take some extra cases for the doctor. The war looks bad, doesn't it? They need surgeons and though I'm doing something in patching up these poor fellows and sending them back, I wonder often if I oughtn't to go into a war hospital. Do you remember the little cameo pin you used to wear till father thought it was too dressy for you? If you haven't lost it, I wish you'd send it down here for me to pawn. I can get it back after the war. I think of you often though I don't write. Don't work too hard.

"Your loving son,
"JASON."

"Sept. 24, 1862.

"DEAR MOTHER:

"Could you possibly sell something to get five dollars to me by return packet? Will write fully later.

"Your loving son,
"JASON."

But there was nothing more to sell.

"My dear boy," wrote Jason's mother, "I am heartbroken, for I know how hard you are working, but truly, I have nothing left of the least value. The cameo pin was the last. Am very much worried lest you are sick. Do let me know. I am very well and the neighbors are kind. Pilgrim is well, too, though the scar is there on his shoulder. I'm sure he will always remember what you did for him. He is all but human. *Please* write me.

"A hug and kiss, from Mother."

Jason's fourth letter was urgent and prompt in reply.

"DEAR MOTHER:

"I am going into the army, mother. The need for surgeons is urgent and I've got to help lick the South. I thought, barring the five from you, I could raise enough to buy into practice with Dr.

Edwards before I leave, so that if I live, I will have that to return to. It will cost a hundred dollars. But I can't do it. So I guess you'll have to sell Pilgrim. I hate to ask it of you but after all he's only an expense to you and I'll buy you another, after the war. Sell him to the government for an army horse. Mr. Inchpin will attend to it for you.

> "Lovingly,
> "JASON."

Jason's mother read the letter with tears running down her cheeks. It was November. Drearily the Kentucky hills rolled back from the river and drearily the Ohio valleys stretched inland. Pilgrim plodded patiently toward the stable and his mistress, huddled in the saddle, gave him no heed until Pilgrim stamped impatiently at the stable door. Then she dismounted and the great horse stamped into his stall.

"O Pilgrim," she sobbed, "Jason is going to war. Jason is going to war. I can't lose him too!"

The horse turned his fine head and nickered softly as he rubbed his soft nose on her shoulder.

"And I've got to let you go, old friend," she added. "I know that I don't need you, Pilgrim. It's just that you are like a living bit of father—and if Jason would only seem to understand that, it wouldn't be so hard to let you go. I wonder if all young folks are like Jason?"

Old Pilgrim leaned his head over his stall and in the November gloaming he looked long at his mistress with his wise and gentle eyes. It was as if he would tell her that he had learned that youth is always a little hard; that only long years in harness with always the back-breaking load to pull, not for oneself, but for others, can make the really grateful heart. One of the sweet, deep compensations of the years, the gray horse seemed to say, is that gratitude grows in the soul.

So Jason and Old Pilgrim both went to war. They did not see each other, but each one, in his own way, made a brilliant record. Pilgrim learned the sights and sounds and smells of war. The fearful pools of blood ceased to send him plunging and rearing in harness. The screams of utter fear or of mortal agony no longer set him to neighing or sweating in sympathy. Pilgrim, superb in strength and superb in intelligence, plodded efficiently through a battle just as he had plodded efficiently over the circuit of Jason's Methodist father.

And Jason, cool and clear-headed, with his wonderful long strong hands, sawed and sewed and probed and purged his way through field hospital after field hospital, until the men began to hear of his skill and to ask for him when the fear of death was on them. His work absorbed him more and more, until months went by, and he neglected to write to his mother! Just why, who can say? Each of us looking into his heart, perhaps can find some answer. But Jason was young, and work and world hungry. He did not ask himself embarrassing questions. The months slipped into a year, and the first year into a second year. Still Jason did not write to his mother, nor did he longer hear from her.

In November of the second year Jason was stationed in a hospital near Washington. One rainy morning as he made his way to the cot of a man who was dying of gangrene, an orderly stopped him.

"This is Dr. Jason Wilkins?"

"Yes."

"Sorry, Doctor, but I've got to arrest you and take you to Washington—"

Jason looked the orderly over incredulously. "You've got the wrong man, friend."

The soldier drew a heavy envelop carefully from his breast pocket, and handed it to Jason. Jason opened it uneasily, and gasped. This is what he read: "Show this to Surgeon Jason Wilkins, — — Regiment. Arrest him. Bring him to me immediately.—A. LINCOLN."

Jason whitened. "What's up?" he asked the orderly.

"I didn't ask the President," replied the orderly dryly. "We'll start at once, if you please, Doctor."

In a daze, Jason left for Washington. He thought of all the minor offenses he had committed. But they were only such as any young fellow might have committed. He could not believe that any of them had reached Mr. Lincoln's ears, or that, if they had, the great man in the White House would have heeded them.

Jason was locked in a room in a Washington boarding-house for one night. The next day at noon the orderly called for him. Weak-kneed, Jason followed him up the long drive to the door of the White House, and into a room where there were more orderlies and a man at a desk writing. An hour of dazed waiting, then a man came out of a door and spoke to the man at the desk.

"Surgeon Jason Wilkins," said the sentry.

"Here!" answered Jason.

"This way," jerked the orderly, and Jason found himself in the inner room, with the door closed behind him. The room was empty, yet filled. There was but one man in it besides Jason, but that man was Mr. Lincoln. He sat at a desk, with his somber eyes on Jason's face—still a cool young face, despite trembling knees.

"You are Jason Wilkins?" said Mr. Lincoln.

"Yes, Mr. President," replied the young surgeon.

"Where are you from?"

"High Hill, Ohio."

"Have you any relatives?"

"Only my mother is living."

"Yes, only a mother! Well, young man, how is your mother?"

Jason stammered. "Why, why—I don't know."

"You don't know!" thundered Lincoln. "And why don't you know? Is she living or dead?"

"I don't know," said Jason. "To tell the truth, I've neglected to write and I don't suppose she knows where I am."

There was a silence in the room. Mr. Lincoln clenched a great fist on his desk, and his eyes scorched Jason. "I had a letter from her. She supposes you dead and asked me to trace your grave. What was the matter with her? No good? Like most mothers, a poor sort? Eh? Answer me, sir?"

Jason bristled a little. "The best woman that ever lived, Mr. President."

"Ah!" breathed Mr. Lincoln. "Still you have no reason to be grateful to her! How'd you get your training as a surgeon? Who paid for it? Your father?"

Jason reddened. "Well, no; father was a poor Methodist preacher. Mother raised the money, though I worked for my board mostly."

"Yes, how'd she raise the money?"

Jason's lips were stiff. "Selling things, Mr. President."

"What did she sell?"

"Father's watch—the old silver teapot—the mahogany hat-box—the St. Bartholomew candlestick. Old things mostly; beyond use except in museums."

Again silence in the room, while a look of contempt gathered in Abraham Lincoln's eyes that seared Jason's cool young soul till it scorched him. "You poor fool!" said Lincoln. "You poor worm! Her household treasures—one by one—for you. 'Useless things—fit for museums!' Oh, you fool!"

Jason flushed angrily and bit his lips. Suddenly the President rose and pointed a long, bony finger at his desk. "Come here and sit down and write a letter to your mother!"

Jason stalked obediently over and sat down in the President's seat. Anger and mortification were ill inspirations for letter-writing, but under Lincoln's burning eyes Jason seized a pen and wrote his mother a stilted note. Lincoln paced the floor, pausing now and again to look over Jason's shoulder.

"Address it and give it to me," said the President. "I'll see that it gets to her." Then, his stern voice rising a little: "And now, Jason Wilkins, as long as you are in the army, you write to your mother once a week. If I have reason to correct you on the matter again, I'll have you court-martialed."

Jason rose and handed the letter to the President, then stood, angry and silent, awaiting further orders. Abraham Lincoln took another turn or two up and down the room. Then he paused before the window and looked from it a long, long time. Finally he turned to Jason.

"My boy," he said gently, "there's no finer quality in the world than gratitude. There is nothing a man can have in his heart so mean, so low as ingratitude. Even a dog appreciates a kindness, never forgets a soft word, or a bone. To my mind, the noblest holiday in the world is Thanksgiving. And, next the Creator, there is no one the holiday should be dedicated to as much as to mothers."

Again Lincoln paused, and looked from the boyish face of the young surgeon out of the window at the bleak November skies, and Lincoln said to Jason, with God knows what tragedy of memory in his lonely heart:

> "Freeze, freeze, thou bitter sky,
> Thou dost not bite so nigh
> As benefits forgot."

Another pause. "You may go, my boy." And Lincoln shook hands with Jason, who stumbled from the room, his mind a chaos of resentment and anger. He made his way down Pennsylvania Avenue, pausing as two army officers rode up to a hotel and dismounted, leaving their horses. Something about the big gray that one of the officers rode seemed vaguely familiar to the young doctor. The gray turned his small, intelligent head toward Jason, then with a sudden soft whinny, laid his head on Jason's shoulder and nuzzled his cheek gently. Jason looked at the right fore shoulder. A three-cornered scar was there. Jason and Old Pilgrim never had met but once, and yet—Jason was little more than a boy. Suddenly he threw his arms around Old Pilgrim's neck, and sobbed into the silky mane. Passers-by glanced curiously and then went on. Washington was full of tears those days.

Pilgrim whinnied and waited patiently. Finally Jason dried his eyes, then stood in thought. The officer who had ridden Pilgrim came out at last. Jason saluted.

"Captain, I'd like to buy that horse from you."

The captain laughed. "There are a number of others like you."

"No, but let me tell you about him, Captain. Give me ten minutes. I'm Dr. Wilkins of — — Hospital."

"O yes, I know of your work. What's the story, Doctor?"

Jason told Pilgrim's history. "She gave him up for me and now I've found him," he finished. "I want to buy him back, get a furlough and take him home to her, myself. I've been saving my money."

"You may have him for just what I paid for him, Doctor," said the captain, who was considerably Jason's senior. "Tell your mother I wish my own mother were living and that I do this in her memory."

"Thank you, sir," said Jason.

A week later Jason led Pilgrim out of the freight car in which he had traveled from Washington to a railway station twenty-five miles from home. The river packets were not running and this was the nearest station to High Hill. It was noon and cold. Jason mounted and started south briskly and once more the Ohio valley opened up before him.

It seemed to Jason that he was seeing the hills for absolutely the first time. And yet that could not be, for back with the first sight of the distant river came all his old boyish reverence for the headlands. The last time he had ridden horseback in the hills had been in the West Virginia circuit, with his father.

For the first time since his interview with the President, Jason began to think of his father. All his newly awakened sense of gratitude had been centered on his mother. Did he then owe his father nothing?

It took courage, it took nerve, it took stomach to patch together the bloody wrecks on the field of battle. It had taken tenacity to an ideal to starve and toil for his profession as he had done in Baltimore. Whence had come these qualities to Jason? He thought once more of his father on that trip on the West Virginian circuit, of the boys expelled from the church, of Sister Clark, of his own sense of mortification and his own contempt. And he dropped his head on his breast with a groan.

And so as the sun set, Pilgrim with the scar on his right fore shoulder and Jason with the scar on his soul that only remorse implants there, stopped before the cottage in High Hill. And through the window, Jason's mother saw them. She rushed to the door and Jason, dismounting, ran up to her, and dropping on his knees, threw his arms about her waist and sobbed against her bosom:

"O mother! O mother! Forgive me! I didn't realize. I didn't know!" Just as many, many sons have done before, and just as many more will do, please God, as long as love and gratitude endure.

Lector House believes that a society develops through a two-fold approach of continuous learning and adaptation, which is derived from the study of classic literary works spread across the historic timeline of literature records. Therefore, we aim at reviving, repairing and redeveloping all those inaccessible or damaged but historically as well as culturally important literature across subjects so that the future generations may have an opportunity to study and learn from past works to embark upon a journey of creating a better future.

This book is a result of an effort made by Lector House towards making a contribution to the preservation and repair of original ancient works which might hold historical significance to the approach of continuous learning across subjects.

HAPPY READING & LEARNING!

LECTOR HOUSE LLP
E-MAIL: lectorpublishing@gmail.com